DATE DUE

GAYLORD			PRINTED IN U.S.A

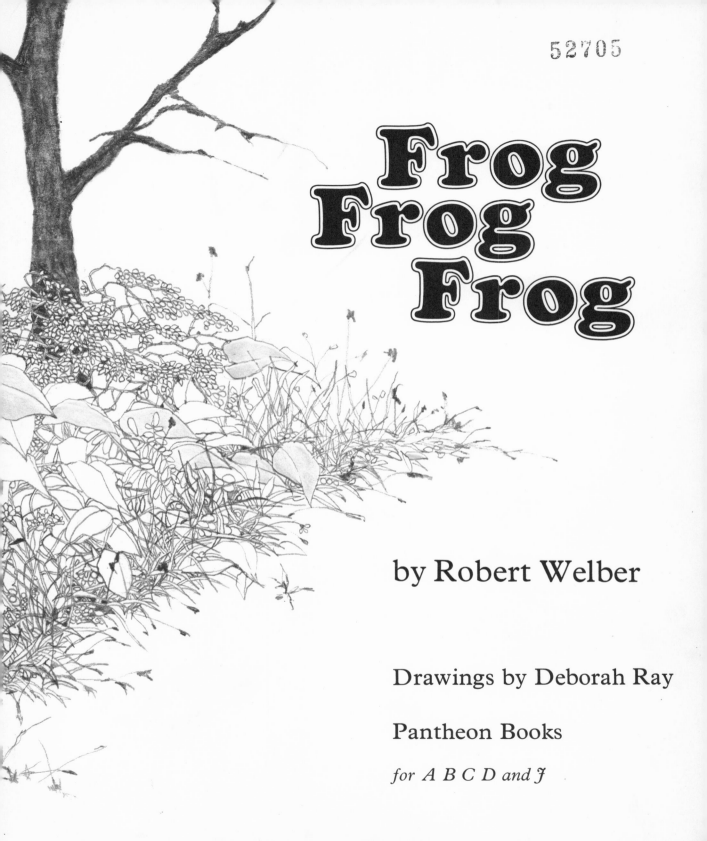

Frog Frog Frog

by Robert Welber

Drawings by Deborah Ray

Pantheon Books

for A B C D and J

"I'm going to catch a frog," Christopher said to his mother.

"You'll have to stand very still and be very quiet," his mother said.

"I can be very still and quiet."

"Good luck," his mother said.

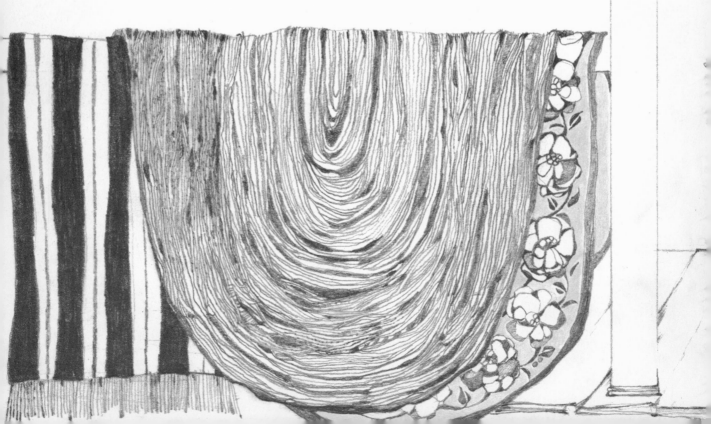

Christopher went outside and began to
crawl around on the ground.
Then he was very still and quiet. He didn't move or
speak for a long time.
He didn't see any frogs.
"Frog, frog, frog," he said. "Come on frog, frog, frog."
He didn't see any frogs.

He began to leap like a frog and he called as he
leaped, "Frog, frog, frog."
He leaped around the trees calling, "Frog,
frog, frog."
He leaped by the flower beds calling, "Frog,
frog, frog."
He leaped by the vegetable garden calling, "Frog,
frog, frog."

He didn't see any frogs.

"I think I will catch a toad," he said.
He ran back to the house.

His mother was in the kitchen feeding the baby.
"I need my net," he told his mother.

He ran to his room. He looked under the bed.
He looked in his closet.
He looked on the porch.
"I can't find my net," Christopher said.
"Look in the bathtub," his mother said.

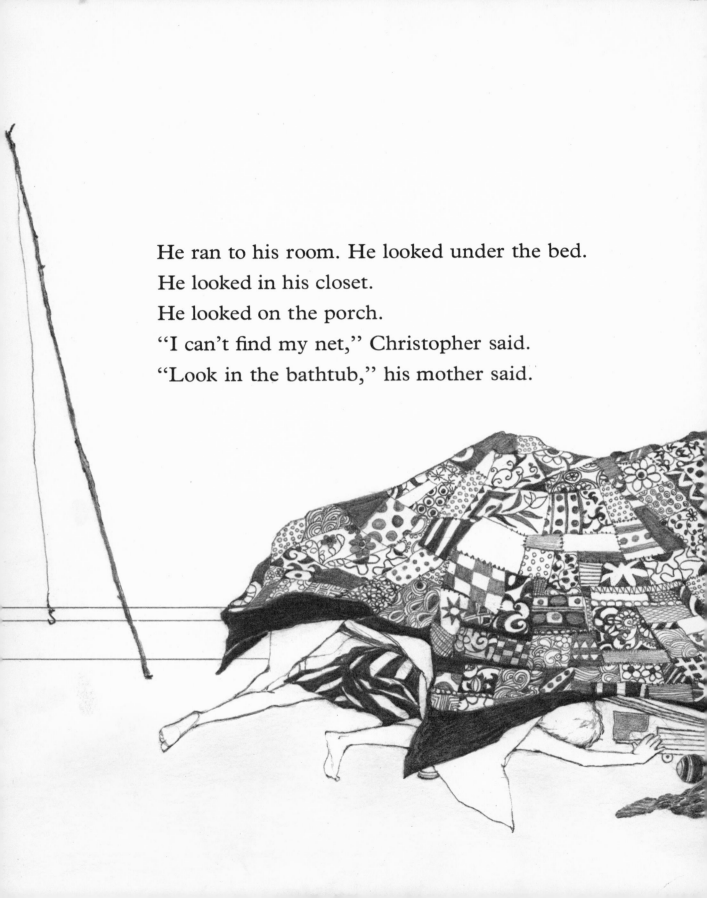

He found his net in the bathtub.

"I'm going to catch a toad," Christopher said to
his mother.
"You'll have to stand very still and be very quiet," his
mother said.
"I can be very still and quiet."
"Good luck," his mother said.

Christopher went outside and began to look
around on the ground holding the net in front of him.
Then he was very still and quiet. He didn't move
or speak for a long, long time.
He didn't see any toads.
"Toad, toad, toad," he said. "Come on toad,
toad, toad."

He didn't see any toads.

He began to leap like a toad and he called as he leaped, "Toad, toad, toad."
He leaped around the trees calling, "Toad, toad, toad."

He leaped by the flower beds calling, "Toad, toad, toad."
He leaped by the vegetable garden calling, "Toad, toad, toad."

He didn't see any toads.

He was very tired and cross. He went
down by the meadow.
He sat where the woods came close by
the meadow.
"Silly old frog," he said. "Silly old toad."
He threw his net down beside him and stared into
the woods. He did not move or speak for
a long, long, long time.

Then he saw the frog leaping near the tree.

Then he saw the toad leaping near the frog.
Then he saw the tiny, tiny frogs and tiny, tiny
toads jumping, jumping all around the big frog
and big toad.
They moved from the sunshine into the shadow
of the woods.
He watched them as they jumped. He watched
them for a long, long, long, long time.

Then he went running home, running across the meadow,
running by the vegetable garden,
running by the flower beds,
running by the trees.

"Did you catch a frog?" his mother asked him.
"No," Christopher said. "I saw them. They were
jumping into the woods. They were with their mothers.
Some of them were this tiny!"
"Is that so," his mother said. "Why didn't you
catch them?"
"It would have ruined their jump," Christopher said.
"Come on. I'll show you."

He took her hand and led her and the baby in her arms down to the meadow to the edge of the woods.

He didn't see any frogs or toads.

"They have gone away," he said to his mother.

"Perhaps they have gone home," she said.

"I didn't catch any," Christopher said.

"It would have ruined their jump," he said.

His mother kissed him on the cheek.

They stood a while looking into the woods.
Then they walked home across the meadow.